Disney's
Winnie the Pooh
Time
for
School,
Pooh

By Kathleen W. Zoehfeld
Illustrated by Robbin Cuddy

A Random House PICTUREBACK® Book

Copyright © 1997, 2001 by Disney Enterprises, Inc. Based on the Pooh stories by A. A. Milne (Copyright The Pooh Properties Trust).
All rights reserved under International and Pan-American Copyright Conventions. Published in the United States by Random House, Inc.,
New York, and simultaneously in Canada by Random House of Canada Limited, Toronto, in conjunction with Disney Enterprises, Inc.
Originally published in slightly different form by Disney Press in 1997 as *Pooh's First Day of School.*
Library of Congress Control Number: 00-110036   ISBN: 0-7364-1179-8
www.randomhouse.com/kids/disney
Printed in the United States of America   July 2001   10 9 8 7 6 5 4 3 2 1
PICTUREBACK, RANDOM HOUSE, and the Random House colophon are trademarks of Random House, Inc.

"School is starting! School is starting!" cried Tigger. "Come on! Don't be late!"

"School?" asked Winnie the Pooh. "What are you talking about?"

"Christopher Robin has a new backpack and lunch box, and he's getting ready for school. We'd better get ready too!"

"School is for children," said Pooh. "Not for tiggers and bears of little brains."

"What do you mean, not for us?" asked Tigger.
"Tiggers LOVE to go to school."

"Piglets don't love school," said Piglet thoughtfully. "At least I don't think we do."

"If you ask me," said Eeyore, "school is overrated—with the pencils and whatnot."

"I think it sounds great!" cried little Roo. "Can I go, too?"

"Come along, Roo," said Pooh. "We'll all go see Christopher Robin. Maybe he can tell us more about it."

"Where's the school?" Tigger asked as soon as he saw
Christopher Robin.

"It's about a mile away," said Christopher Robin. "The school bus will come tomorrow morning to take me there."

"A mile?" asked Piglet.

"It's not here in the Hundred-Acre Wood?" asked Tigger.

"If you have to go that far from home, I'm sure school is not a good thing for piglets," said Piglet, nervously tugging at his ear.

"We don't have the brains for it anyway," said Pooh.

"You'd all like school," said Christopher Robin. "I'm sure of it! Wait here a moment, and I'll make a classroom just for us."

"Oh, my! Our very own school!" said Pooh. "I hope we like it."

"Can we bounce in school?" asked Roo.

"Of course you can, little buddy!" said Tigger.

"School's the bounciest place there is!"

"There's no bouncing in school,"
said Eeyore decisively.

"None?" asked Tigger.

"School is work. No
time for fun," said Eeyore.

"No fun?" said Tigger in
a low voice. "Maybe tiggers
don't like school after all."

Tigger and Piglet were about to tiptoe away when
Christopher Robin called out, "Time for school to begin!"

Christopher Robin set up a table and chairs that were just the right size for his friends.

"We always start the day by singing a song," said Christopher Robin. *"Welcome, all children, good morning to you. . . .* Now everyone join in!"

"*Good morning,*" they all sang.

"Piglet," whispered Pooh, "don't you think this is fun?"

"The first day of school can be hard," said Christopher Robin. "But my teacher is really nice. And I know two friends who will be in my class."

"It's nice to spend your days with friends," said Piglet.

"And we learn things in school, too," said Christopher Robin.

"Do you think we can learn anything?" Pooh asked Piglet.

"I hope so," answered Piglet.

"You can learn to write your ABCs," said Christopher Robin. "It's fun."

Christopher Robin handed out paper and crayons to everyone.

"The best letters of the alphabet are the letters in our own names," said Christopher Robin. "Let's all draw pictures of ourselves and write our names on them."

Christopher Robin helped Pooh print "P-O-O-H" with a purple crayon.

Piglet, whose name was really quite complicated, printed "P-T."

"Very nice!" cried Christopher Robin.

Eeyore, who knew only the letter A, wrote "A" under his picture. "Don't know when I've had so much fun,"  he said proudly. Roo made some  quotation marks. Tigger made a squiggle.  Everyone did a fine job.

"Counting is easy, too," said Christopher Robin.
"Pooh, let's see how high you can stack some blocks."

"1, 2, 3, 4, 5," Pooh counted as he built a lovely
tower. But when tiggers see towers, they think, "Towers
are for bouncing," and . . .

CRASH! Down went the blocks.

"Oh," sighed Pooh.

"Tigger!" said Christopher Robin sternly.

"Sorry," said Tigger. "ABCs and 1-2-3s are fine, but what about fun? What good is a place if you can't even bounce in it?"

"You can't bounce when your teacher is talking," said Christopher Robin, "but my school has a playground and we get to play in it nearly every day."

"I knew tiggers loved school!" cried Tigger.

When Pooh's tummy started to feel a bit rumbly, he worried about something else. "I hope you're allowed to eat at school," he said.

"Oh, yes," said Christopher Robin. "That's what my new lunch box is for. I'm going to bring a peanut-butter-and-honey sandwich, a banana, and milk."

"*Mmmm,*" sighed Pooh.

And then Christopher Robin, who knew his friend very well, said, "Why don't we have a little snack right now?"

He set out a large pot of honey, and everyone had some.

"Christopher Robin, I hope your new teacher is as nice as you are," said Piglet.

"Yes!" agreed Pooh. "Can we play school again tomorrow?"

"PLEASE?!" cried all the rest.

"Of course," said Christopher Robin. "We'll play every day—as soon as I'm home from school."